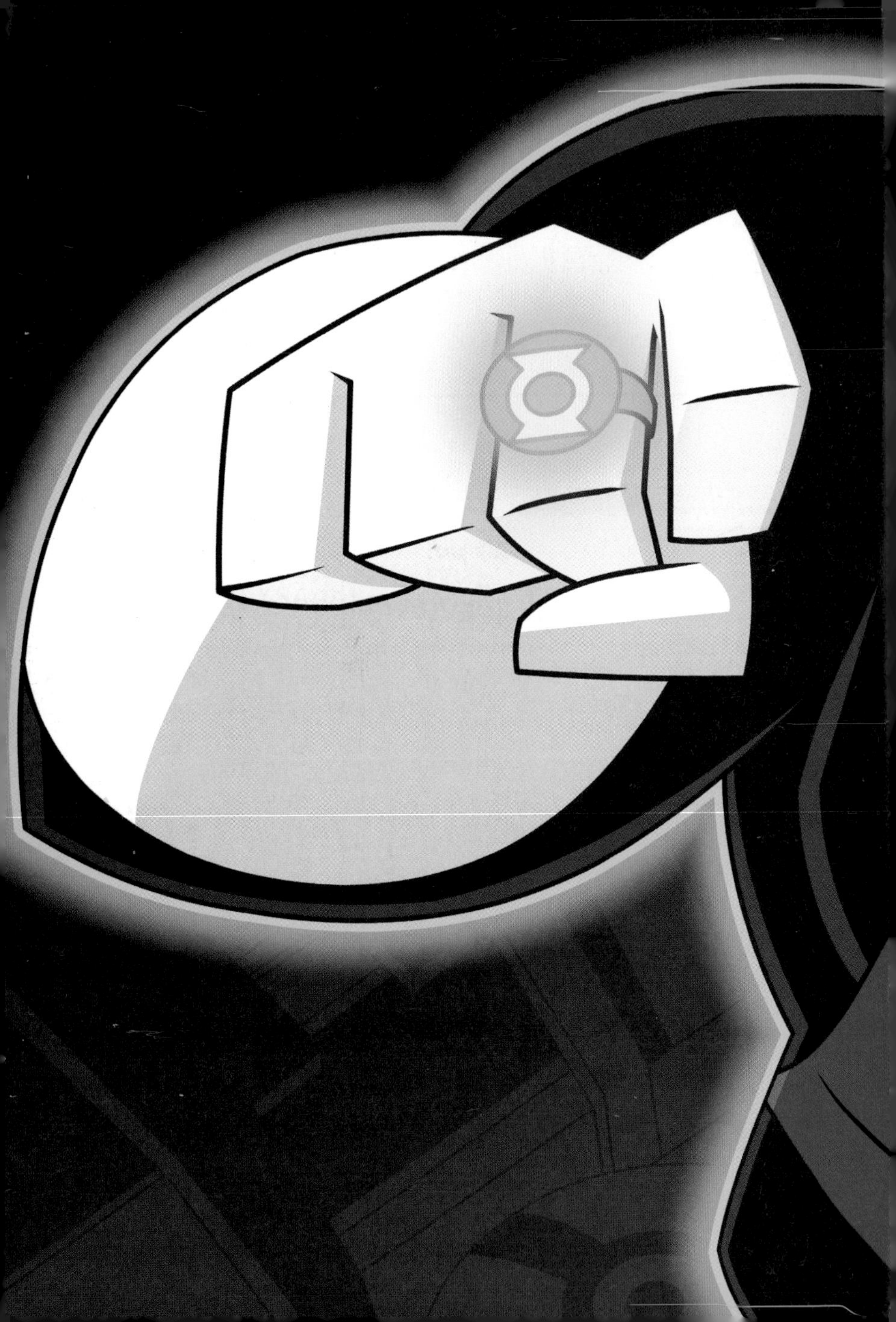

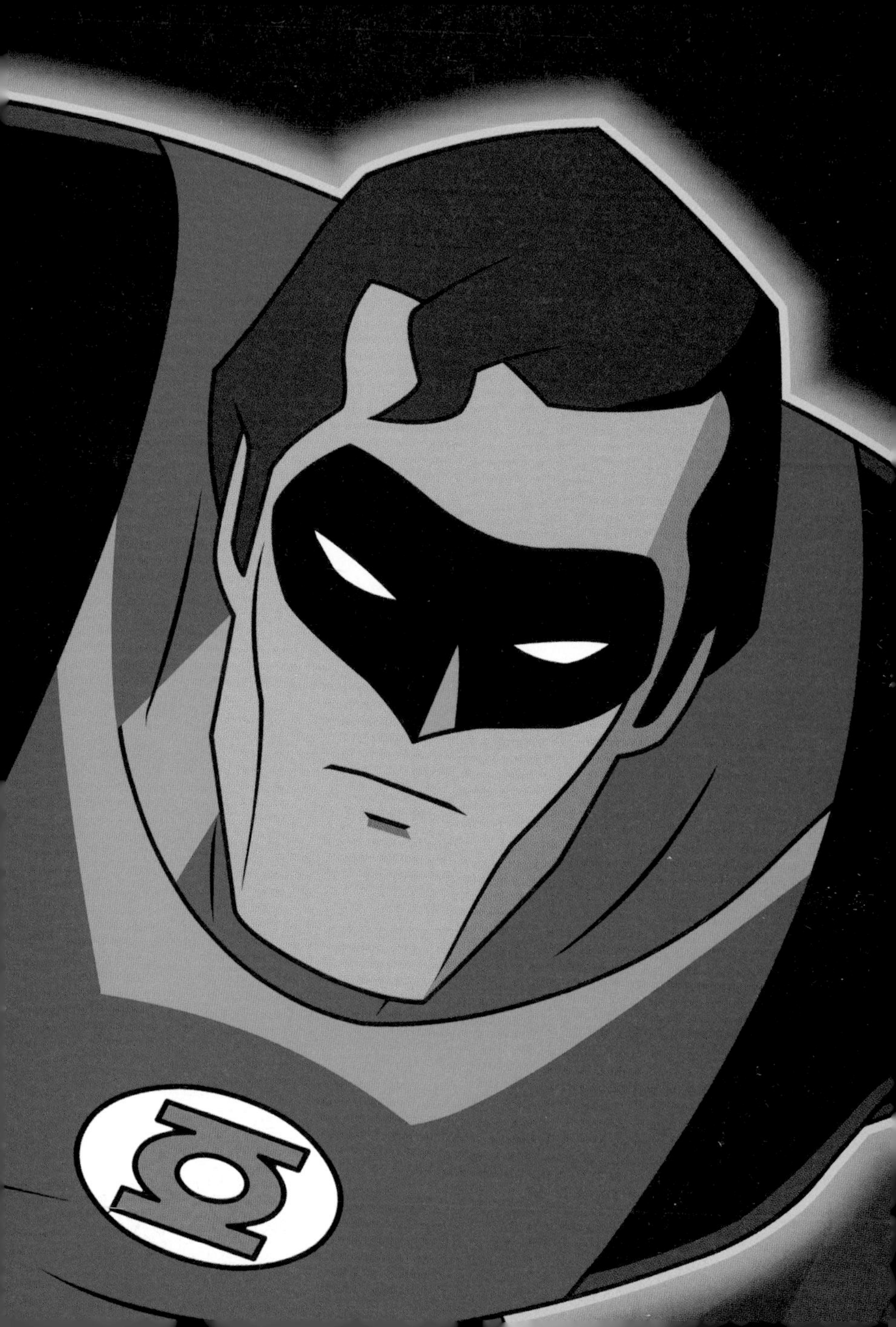

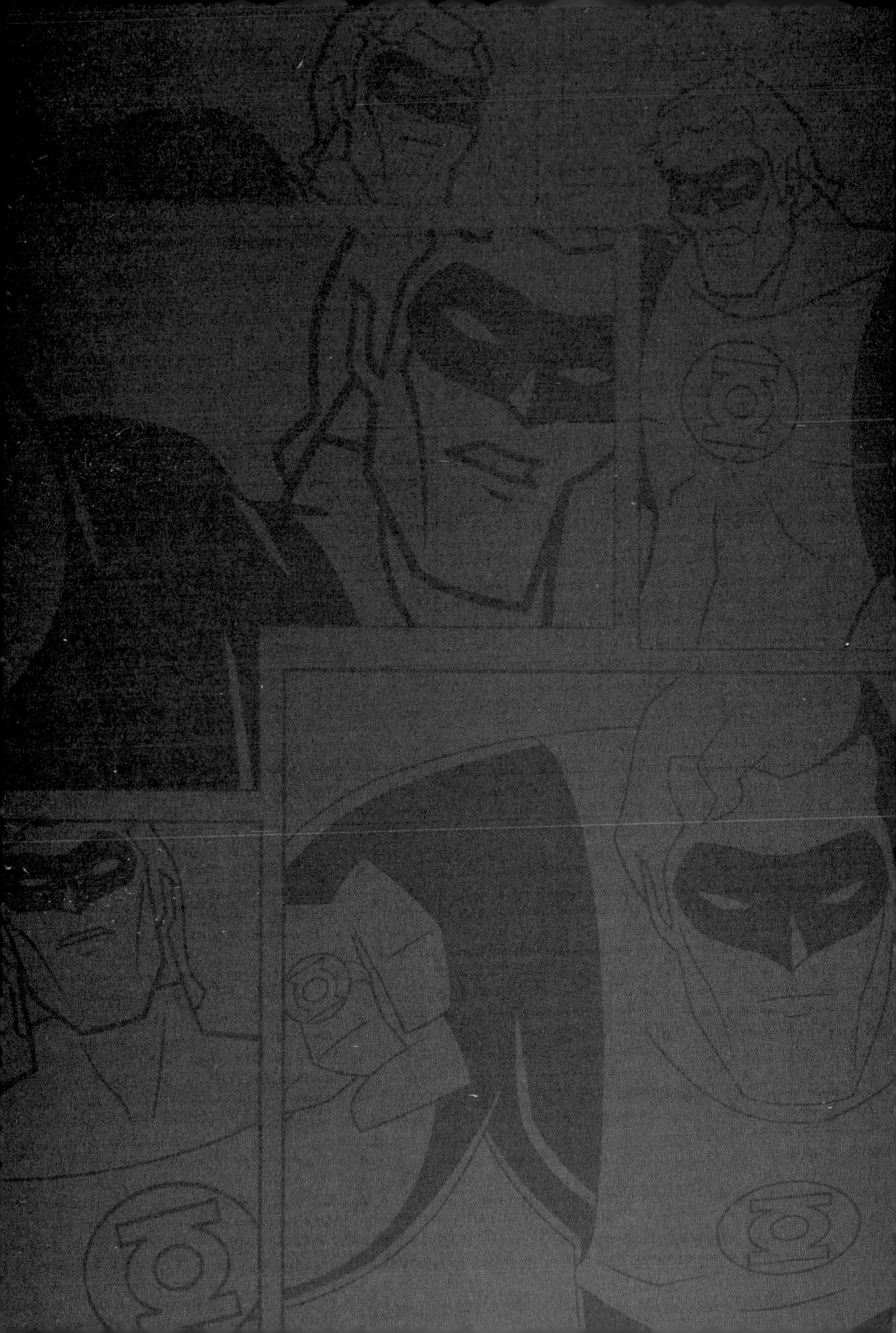

AS THE NEWEST MEMBER OF AN INTERGALACTIC PEACEKEEPING FORCE KNOWN AS THE GREEN LANTERN CORPS, HAL JORDAN FIGHTS EVIL AND PROUDLY WEARS THE UNIFORM AND RING OF . . .

SUPER DC HEROES™

GREEN LANTERN

PRISONER OF THE RING

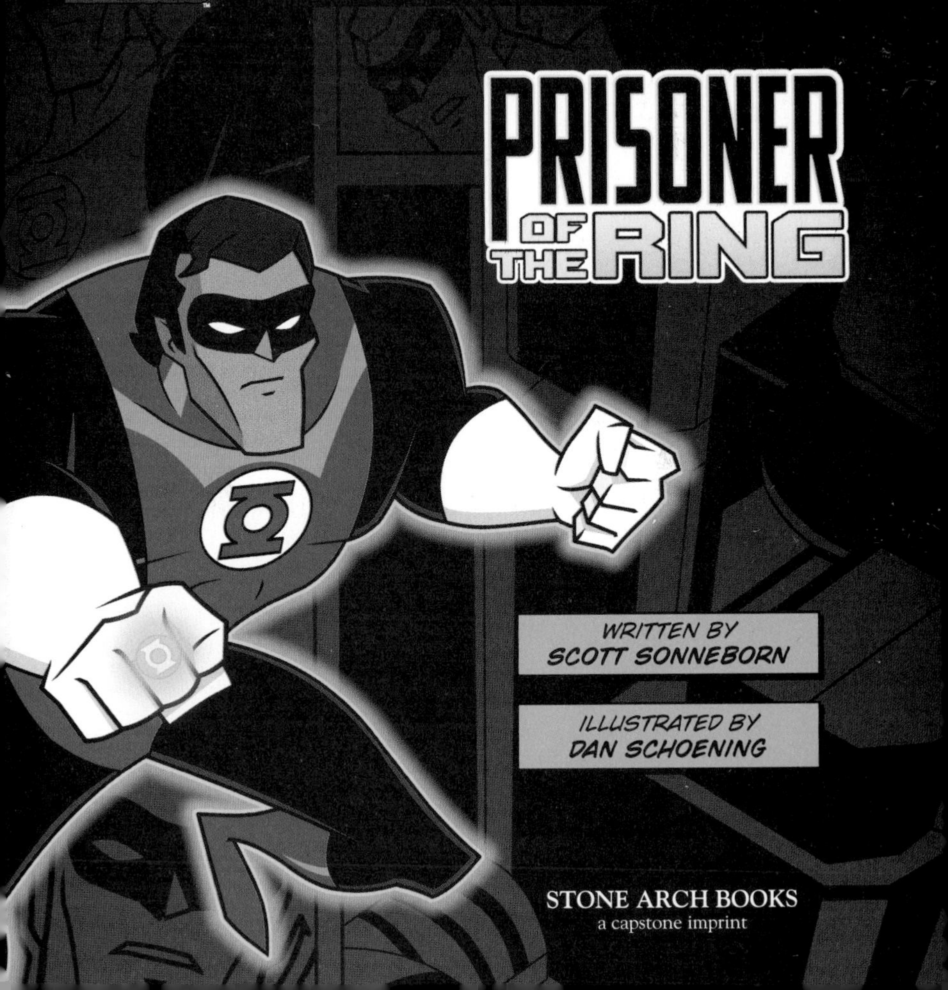

WRITTEN BY
SCOTT SONNEBORN

ILLUSTRATED BY
DAN SCHOENING

STONE ARCH BOOKS
a capstone imprint

Published by Stone Arch Books in 2012
A Capstone Imprint
151 Good Counsel Drive, P.O. Box 669
Mankato, Minnesota 56002
www.capstonepub.com

Library of Congress Cataloging-in-Publication Data
Sonneborn, Scott.
  Prisoner of the ring / written by Scott Sonneborn ; illustrated by Dan
Schoening.
    p. cm. -- (DC super heroes)
  ISBN-13: 978-1-4342-2624-2 (library binding)
  ISBN-13: 978-1-4342-3410-0 (pbk.)
  1. Green Lantern (Fictitious character)--Juvenile fiction. 2. Superheroes--
Juvenile fiction. 3. Supervillains--Juvenile fiction. [1. Superheroes--Fiction. 2.
Supervillains--Fiction. 3. Wizards--Fiction. 4. Science fiction.] I. Schoening,
Dan, ill. II. Title.
  PZ7.S6982Pr 2012
  813.6--dc22   2011005150

Summary: An evil wizard has escaped from the Sciencell prison on the planet
Oa. Using a powerful magic spell, the sorcerer has located the perfect hideout:
Green Lantern's ring! Hal Jordan must shrink to microscopic size and enter the
ring itself, or else his unlimited power will turn against the very galaxies he has
sworn to protect.

Art Director: Bob Lentz and Brann Garvey
Designer: Hilary Wacholz
Production Specialist: Michelle Biedscheid

Printed in the United States of America in Stevens Point, Wisconsin.
082011
006349R

TABLE OF CONTENTS

CHAPTER 1

MESSAGE IN SPACE..................4

CHAPTER 2

BREAK OUT! 13

CHAPTER 3

KILLER COPY.......................21

CHAPTER 4

LAVA MONSTER.....................30

CHAPTER 5

OUTSMARTED 40

MESSAGE IN SPACE

WHOOOOSH!

The asteroid zoomed right at Hal Jordan. He was deep in space and millions of miles away from any help. But the super hero was far from helpless.

Hal was a Green Lantern. The ring he wore was one of the most powerful weapons in the galaxy. Hal used it to create a giant green jackhammer. It smashed through the asteroid. The big space rock shattered into a thousand harmless pieces.

Hal turned back to the ugly spaceship floating in front of him. "So who's inside?" Hal asked his ring.

"The crew call themselves the Interstellar Privateers," the ring informed him.

Hal had never been a great student, but remembered enough from English class to know that "privateers" was a fancy word for pirates. There was nothing fancy about these guys, though. They were mean. They were thieves. And their ship's cannons were firing asteroids like they were cannonballs!

Two more flew straight at Hal. He willed his ring to create two giant slides. Each slide caught one of the asteroids and sent it sliding into the other.

KA-BOOM! The asteroids crashed together and crushed each other into dust.

"Attention," chirped Hal's ring. "You are receiving a message."

"Put the call through," said Hal as the Privateers fired another asteroid. He smashed it with a giant sledgehammer.

As always, the ring instantly did what Hal commanded.

"Hal, it's Voz," said a voice over Hal's ring. Voz was a Green Lantern, but one with a special job. Instead of protecting a space sector like Hal did, Voz was the warden of the Sciencells on Oa.

Oa was the home of the Green Lantern Corps. It held their headquarters, their training grounds, and the Sciencells — the most advanced prison in the universe.

"I'm having a little trouble with one of my prisoners," continued Voz.

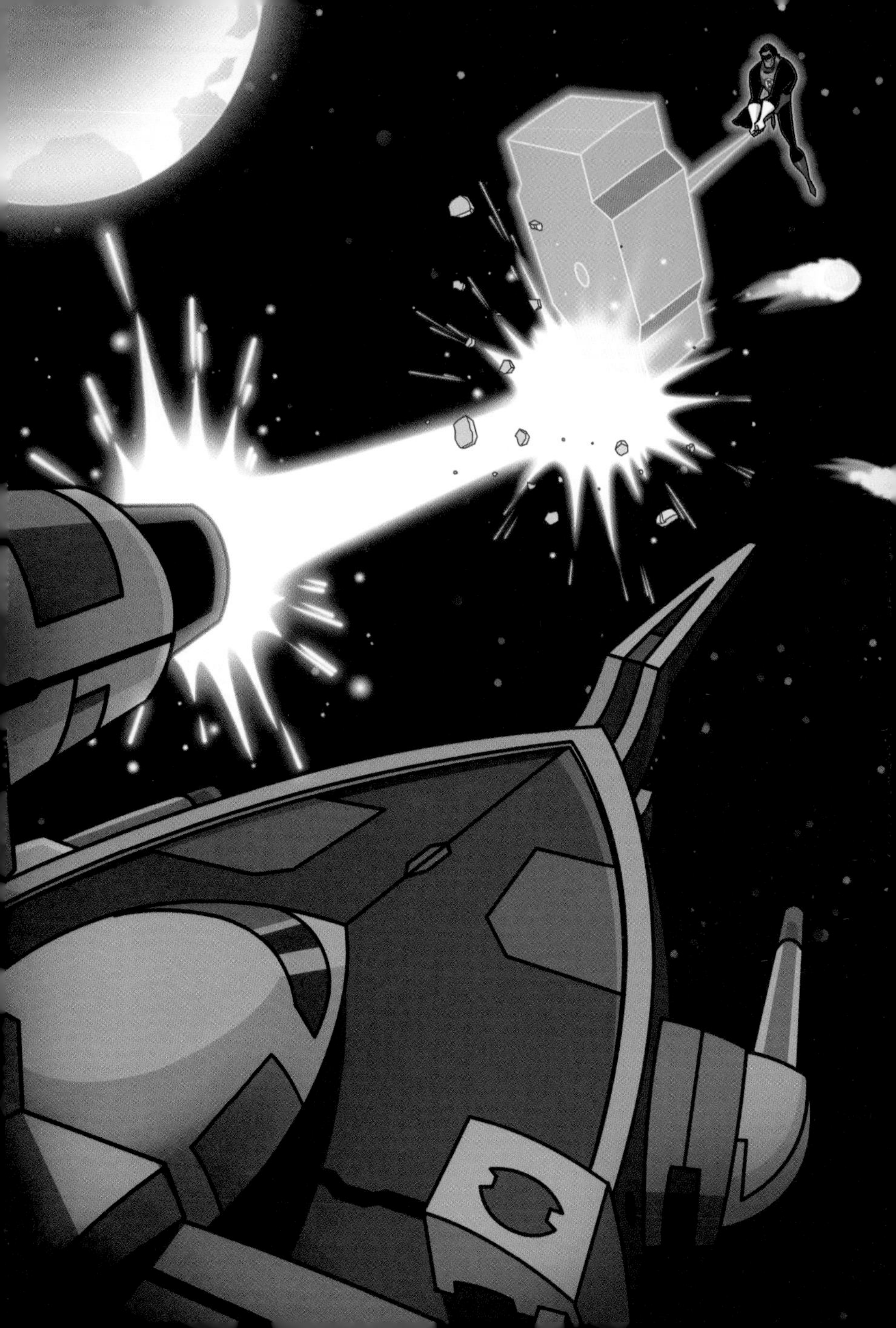

"Can you hold a second?" asked Hal.

BOOM! BOOM! BOOM!

The Privateers fired all their cannons at once. Dozens of asteroids flew at Hal. There was no way Hal could smash them all.

Instead, Hal silently commanded his ring to create a tennis racket that was as big as a skyscraper. When the asteroids hit the racket's net, they bounced right back. Several of them smashed into the engine of the Privateers' ship.

"Sorry to interrupt, Voz," said Hal. "You were saying something about a prisoner?"

"It's Myrwhydden," replied Voz. "Since you're the one who caught him, I'm hoping you can help."

"Already on my way," said Hal. He flew toward Oa, dragging the ship behind.

When Hal first became a Green Lantern and traveled to other planets, he wasn't surprised to find that many of them were filled with advanced science.

What he didn't expect to find in outer space was magic. Myrwhydden was the most powerful wizard on his home planet. He was also the most evil. Hal had been caught by surprise when he discovered that, somehow, Myrwhydden had gotten inside his power ring. Hal then used his ring to shrink himself down, so he could follow the wizard inside.

Their battle in the ring was fierce. Hal gave it everything he had. Even that almost wasn't enough. Myrwhydden was a mighty sorcerer. He was also very smart. That was his greatest strength.

It was also his biggest weakness.

"Myrwhydden thinks he's smarter than everyone else, including me," remembered Hal. "Actually, make that *especially* me!"

Myrwhydden never imagined that an earthling like Hal would be able to outsmart him. Which is exactly why Hal was able to do it. Hal defeated the wizard and imprisoned him in a Sciencell. That was the last Hal had heard of Myrwhydden.

Until now.

When Hal landed on Oa, the ape-like Voz was there to greet him. "What's that?" asked Voz, pointing to the Privateers' ship.

Hal smiled. "I figured if I was going to visit the warden of the Sciencells, I might as well bring a present," said Hal. "You might want to wait until we're inside the cells to unwrap it, though."

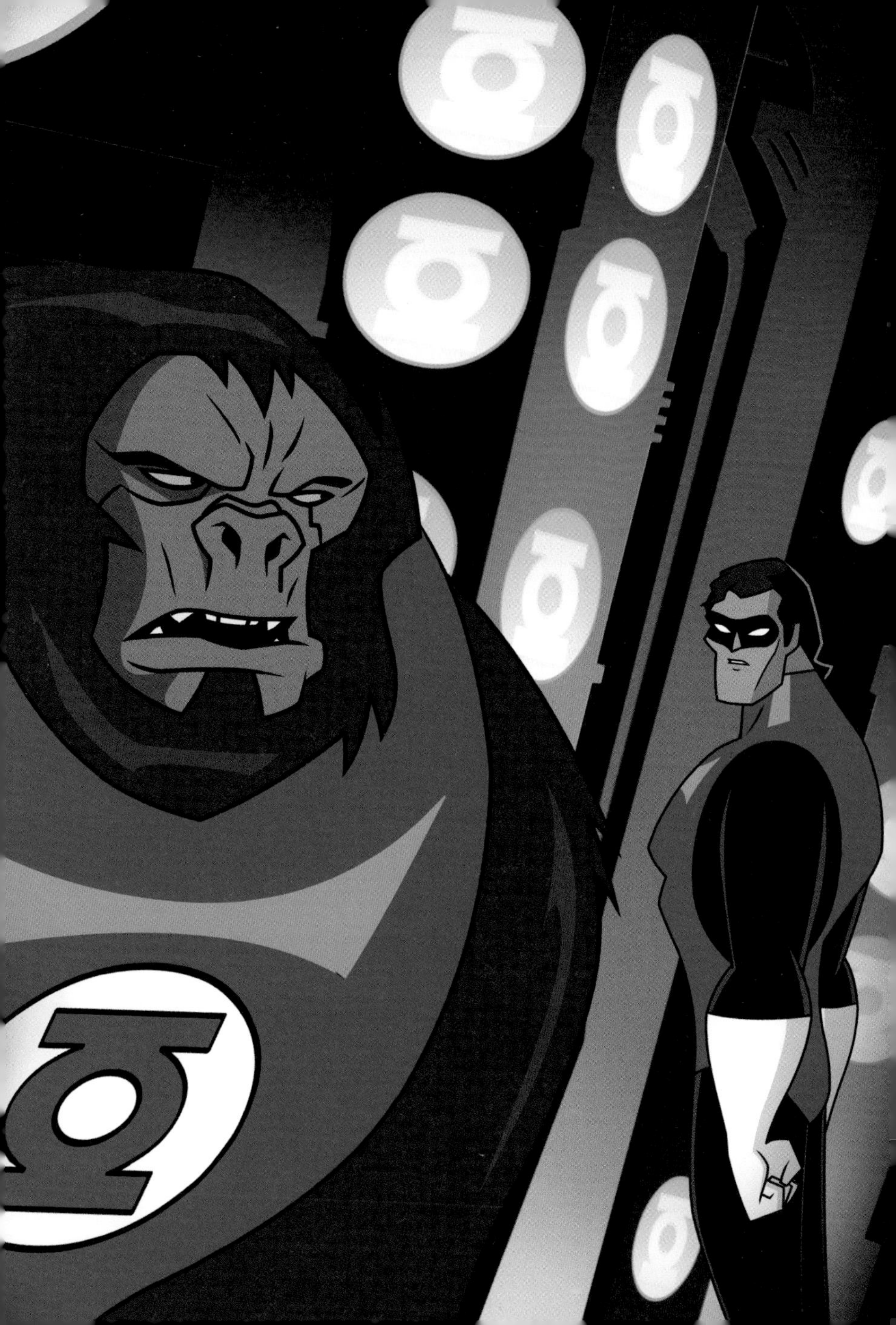

Voz took Hal through the impressive security doors and into the Sciencells. The cells held some of the deadliest villains in the galaxy. Hal saw Grayven, Lyssa Drak, and other creatures that were even more evil and more hideous.

Voz put the Privateers into a Sciencell. Then together, the two Green Lanterns flew to Myrwhydden's cell.

But the evil wizard was gone!

CHAPTER 2

BREAK OUT!

"That's impossible!" cried Voz. "The cell containing Myrwhydden was designed to drain all of his magical powers. He couldn't have cast a spell in there."

"Then how did he escape —?" asked Hal. **ZzZAPPPPPPP!** A sudden blast sent Voz reeling off his feet.

Hal was shocked to see Voz fall to the ground. Hal was even more surprised to see where the blast had come from.

It had been fired from Hal's own ring!

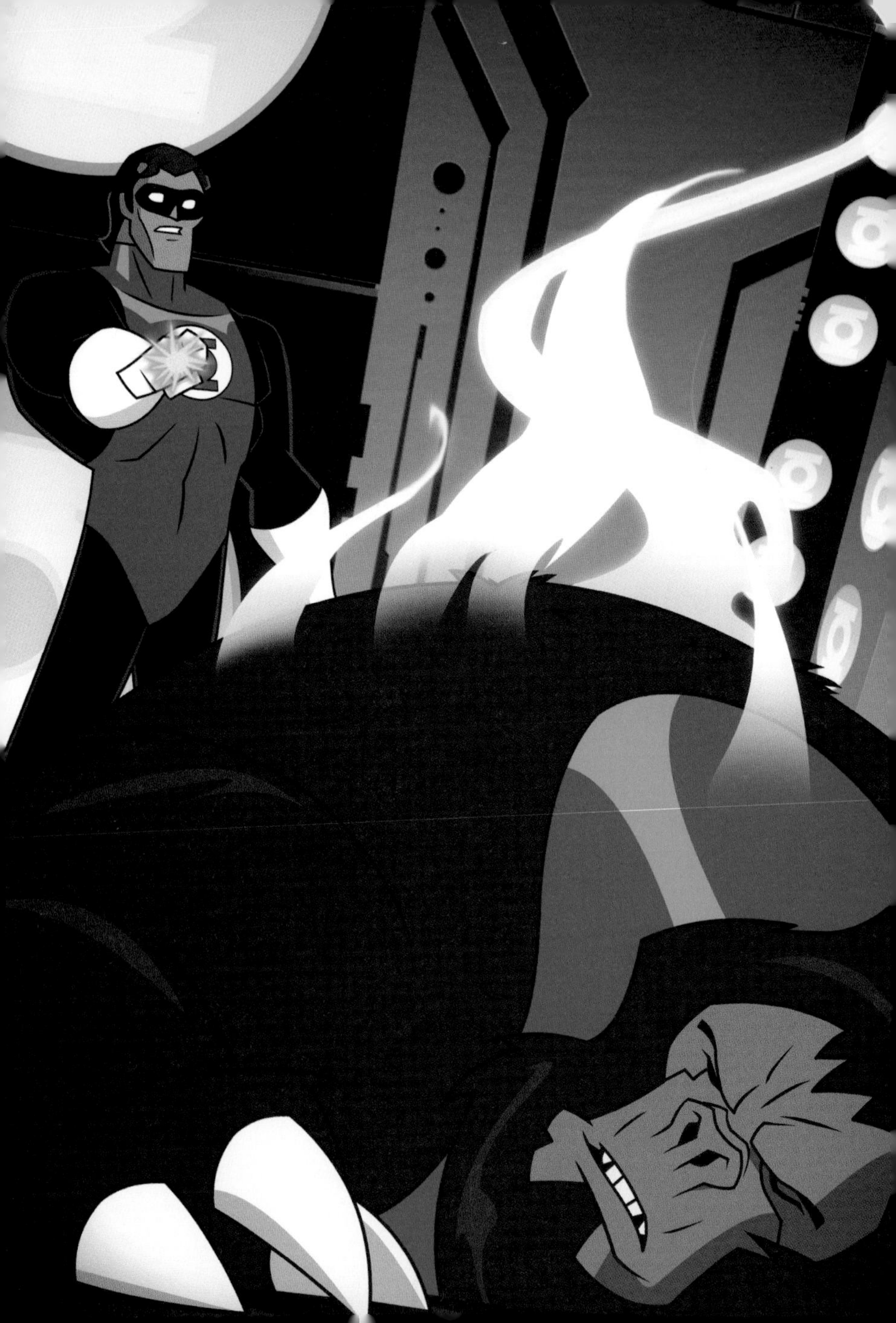

"Why did you do that?" Hal asked his power ring.

"Like I'd tell you?" replied the ring.

Hal couldn't believe it. His ring had just talked back to him. It had never done anything like that before.

"What's going on?" demanded Hal.

"Oh, will you please shut up!" said the ring. "I'm busy here!"

Suddenly, Hal recognized that voice. It wasn't the ring. It was . . .

"Myrwhydden!" yelled Hal. "I don't know how you got back in my ring, but —"

"Of course you don't know how I did it!" interrupted Myrwhydden from inside the ring. "How could you? You are nowhere near as intelligent as I am!"

Hal ignored the insult. Now wasn't the time to argue with the wizard.

"In fact," continued Myrwhydden, "you never would have defeated me in the first place, if I hadn't had a cold that day!"

"You seemed perfectly fine to me," Hal couldn't help reply. "Until I beat you!"

Hal immediately wished he hadn't said that. What he needed to do was get Myrwhydden back in his cell. Making the wizard mad wouldn't help.

"You have a bad memory," shouted Myrwhydden. "That's yet another sign of a weak brain! Not that I need more proof. After all, you had no idea I planted a spell inside your ring when I was there before. The spell allows me to get inside the ring if you are ever within a few yards of me."

"You were also completely fooled when I used Voz to trick you into coming here, so you'd be close enough to trigger the spell," added Myrwhydden. "Which is yet another example of me outsmarting you!"

"Okay, okay, I get it. You've got a big brain," groaned Hal. Myrwhydden was getting on Hal's nerves. "You also have a big head! I hope you're having fun bragging about what you've done so far, because that's all you're going to do. Even inside my ring, you'll never be able to escape from Oa."

"Oh, I don't plan to," replied the wizard from inside the ring. "At least, not alone."

Hal looked down and saw his ring glow hot with power. **ZZZRRRRTT!** It blasted a beam of green energy at the locked Sciencells.

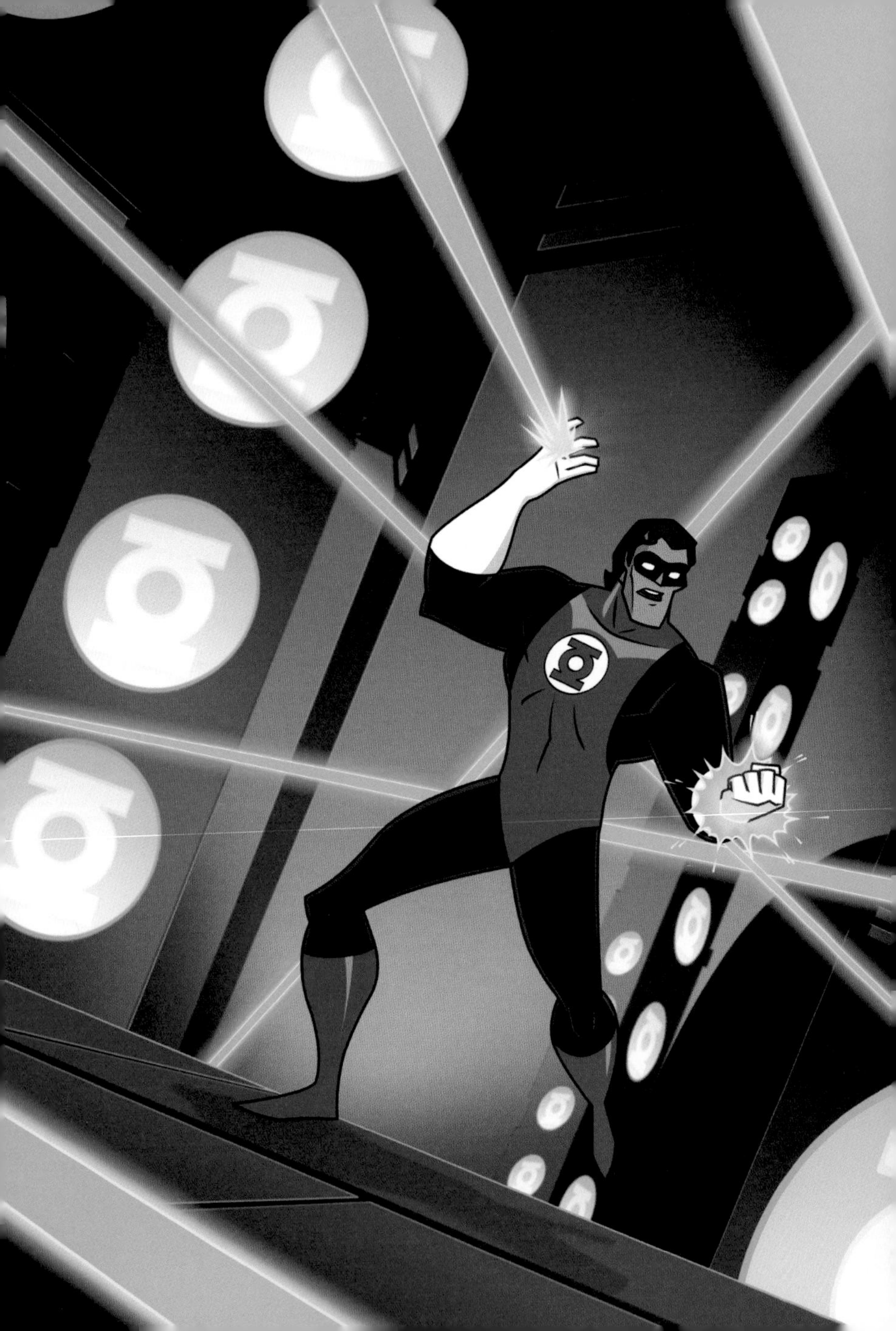

"What are you doing?" cried Hal.

"Do you need me to spell out everything for you?" shouted Myrwhydden. "I'm using your ring to free all the other criminals!"

Hal's eyes went wide. If any one of those villains escaped, millions of lives could be at risk. If they all got out at the same time, the entire universe was in danger.

ZZRRRRRTT! Hal's ring kept blasting away. Hal willed it to stop, but the ring ignored his command.

"Having a little trouble with your ring?" asked Myrwhydden. "That's probably because it isn't yours anymore. It's mine!"

It was true. Hal tried to use the ring to call for help, but Myrwhydden blocked the transmission. The wizard wasn't just inside Hal's ring. He was taking control of it.

Hal watched helplessly as Myrwhydden used the ring to seal Voz inside a cube of green energy. Then the wizard had the ring lock the outer doors to the Sciencells and activate the auto-defenses. Now, no one could get inside.

The prison was sealed off from outside help. Hal was on his own. In a few more moments, he would be face-to-face with the deadliest villains in the universe.

CHAPTER 3

KILLER COPY

Few things are more powerful than a Green Lantern ring. But Hal knew it was not simply a weapon. It could do a lot more than just blast things.

Hal quickly scanned through the ring's systems again. Myrwhydden controlled many of the ring's functions, but there was only one thing Hal needed the ring to do right now.

"Shrink me down and send me inside!" Hal ordered the ring.

Hal's body, like every creature in the universe, was made of billions of atoms — with lots of empty space in between. Hal used the ring to push the atoms in his body closer and closer together. As the space between them shrank, so did Hal.

It was delicate work, but Hal didn't have time to be careful. Even as the ring made Hal smaller, it was still blasting away at the Sciencells. There was no time to lose.

Hal shrank faster and faster. He was soon too small to hold the ring on his finger. Hal saw it fall to the floor.

CLINK

The hero took a deep breath and hoped his next one would come inside the ring. If it didn't, then the breath he had just taken would probably be his last.

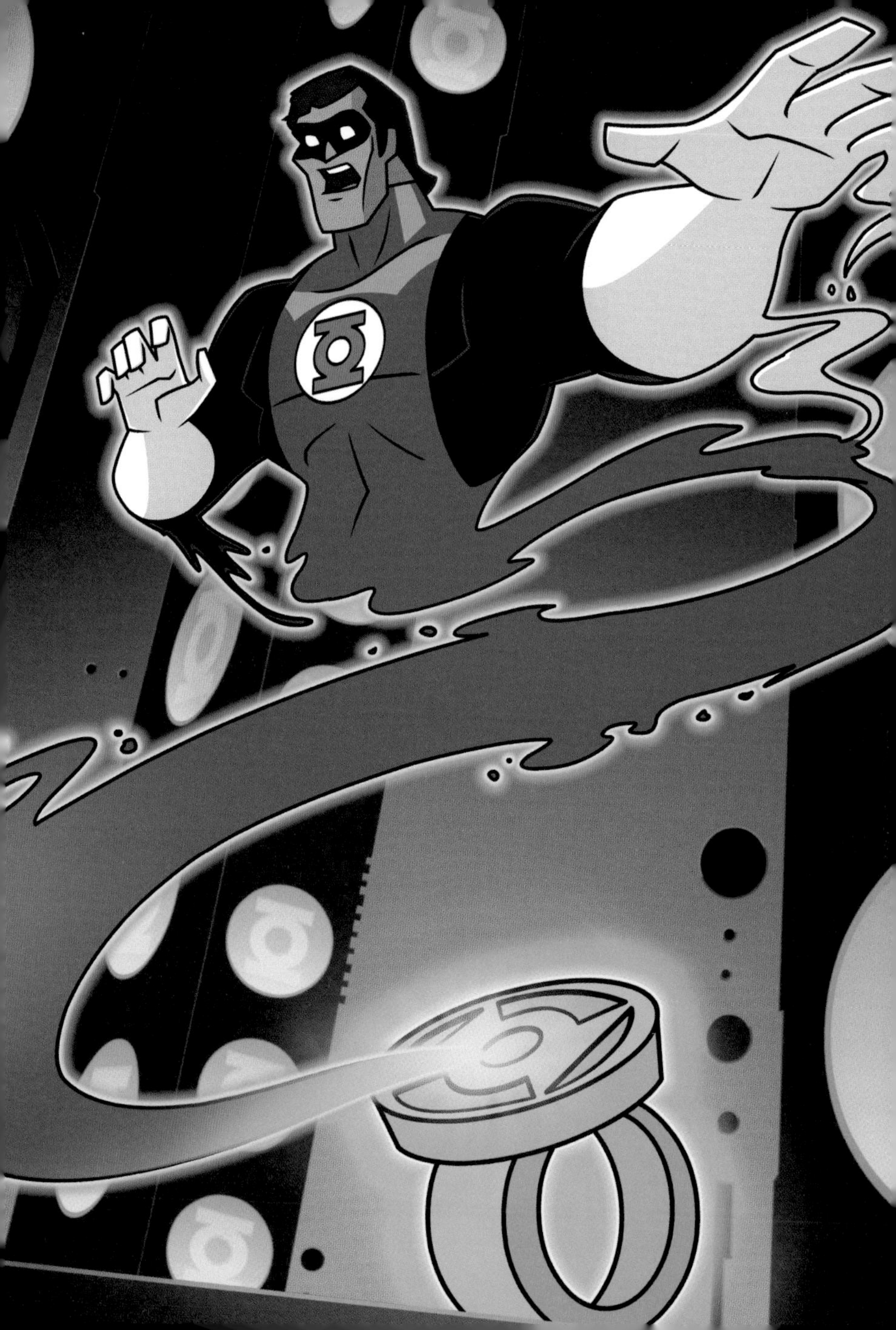

Hal blinked.

Even before opening his eyes, the hero knew he had made it inside. He quickly felt for his ring. It wasn't on his finger.

"Of course it's not there," realized Hal. "I can't wear my ring if I'm inside it."

Hal knew he had to be touching his ring to use it. Then Hal smiled. He may not have been wearing his ring, but he was standing inside it. The ground his boots were touching were part of the ring itself.

Hal thought of a giant telescope — and instantly one appeared.

"Well, at least I can still use the ring to create things," said Hal to himself. "That means I still have a chance to stop Myrwhydden."

If I can find him, thought Hal.

Hal used the telescope to look around. The inside of the ring looked like a giant arena with Hal standing in the middle of it. Thousands of empty seats rose toward a domed ceiling high above him.

"Not what I was expecting," said Hal.

Hal had only been inside his ring once before, when he fought Myrwhydden the first time. Back then, the inside of the ring had looked very different.

"What do you think?" boomed Myrwhydden's voice. He was somewhere inside the ring, but not anywhere that Hal could see. "Now that I'm out of my Sciencell, I've got my magic back. The first thing I did was a little redecorating in here. How does it look?"

"It seems kind of familiar," replied Hal.

"I guess your little brain *does* work," said Myrwhydden. "At least enough to remember somewhere you've been before. I used my magic to recreate a place I found in your ring's data logs. A place called —"

"The Battle Arena of Qward," said Hal, finishing Myrwhydden's sentence.

"Good job, little brain!" said the wizard. "It's going to take a few moments for your ring to open the Sciencells, which means I've got some time to kill, and there's no one I'd rather destroy than you."

Myrwhydden chuckled. "That was a little play on words," he continued. "I suppose it was probably wasted on someone with your limited intelligence."

"Hey, if you're going to keep insulting me," yelled Hal, "at least do it to my face!"

"Oh, please!" said Myrwhydden. "I see what you're trying to do. You think you can trick me?"

"I figured it couldn't hurt to try," Hal said with a shrug.

"That only shows what a fool you are!" roared the wizard. "You're not going to trick me into getting close enough for you to do anything to stop me!"

"He is correct," said a metallic voice. "Such a strategy has less than a one percent chance of success."

Hal turned and saw a 20-foot-tall robot enter the arena. It had gleaming metal skin and a single, evil-looking eye.

"I am Gnaxos," it said.

"I remember Gnaxos," replied Hal. "I fought him when I was on Qward."

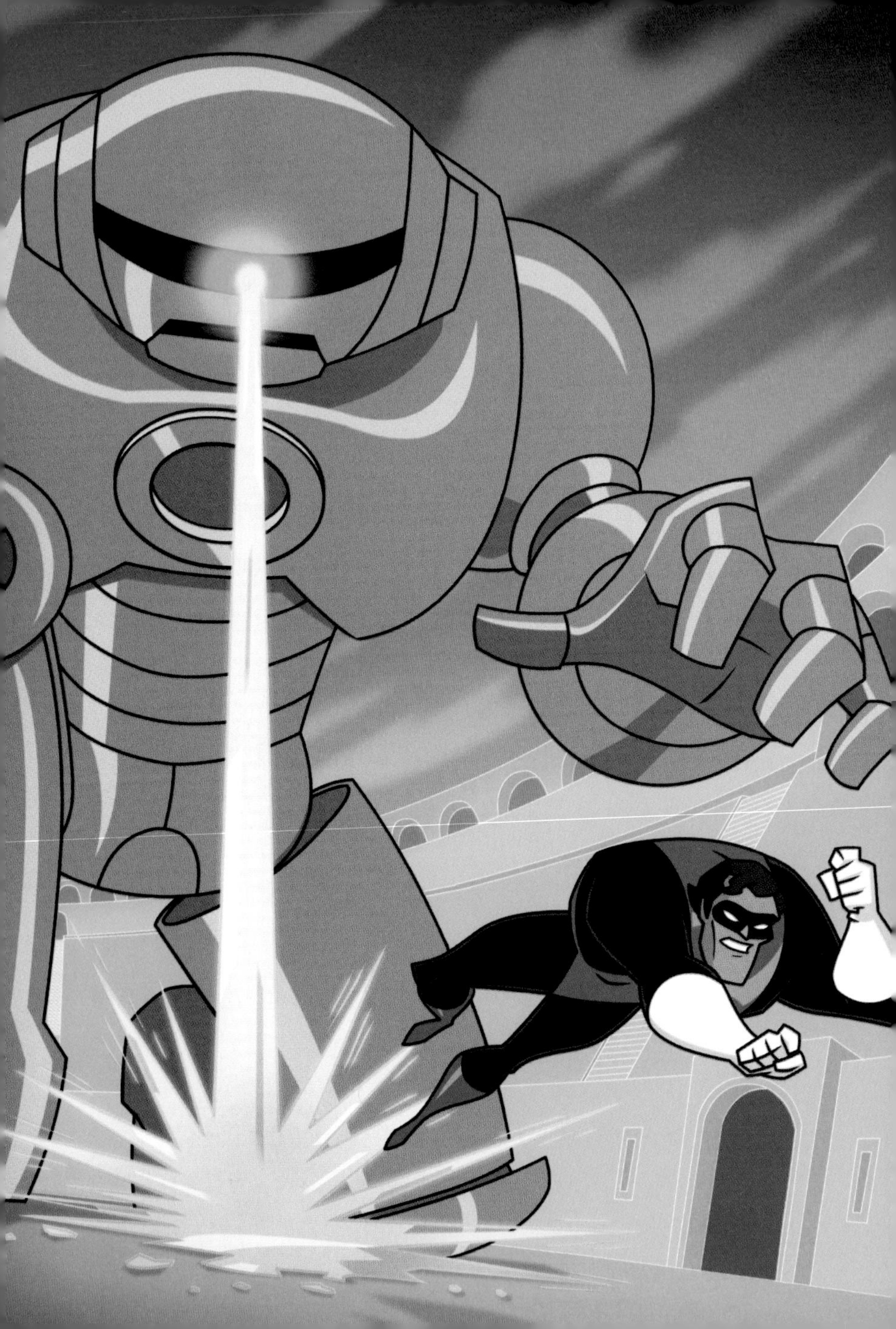

Nothing could pierce his metallic armor, Hal thought. *His eye could shoot fire, ice, and a hundred other things.*

"You're not Gnaxos, though," Hal said. "You're just a copy."

"True, my magic created that robot," said Myrwhydden from wherever he was hiding in the ring. "Still, I think you will find it identical to the original."

"The one who just spoke is correct," stated Gnaxos. Its eye opened wide and fired a blast of ice. THUOOOOMMMMMM!!

Hal dodged, but the robot seemed to know exactly where Hal was going to go. Another blast hit Hal's leg. Instantly, it was covered in ice. Hal couldn't move.

Then Gnaxos' giant shadow fell over him, and everything went dark.

CHAPTER 4

LAVA MONSTER

Hal was completely enclosed inside Gnaxos's giant metal fist. The robot's grip was so tight that no light slipped in between its fingers.

Hal created a giant green crowbar and tried to pry the robot's fist open from the inside. It was no use. Hal was trapped.

"I beat this guy before!" said Hal. "There's got to be a way I can do it again."

Hal thought back to when he had really been on Qward fighting the real Gnaxos.

The giant robot had been incredibly strong. Even worse, it could read Hal's mind. The robot knew what Hal was going to do before he did it.

"Gnaxos saw everything in my head," Hal remembered aloud. "The robot didn't just know how I was going to fight. He knew everything that I knew! He learned that the Green Lanterns are a force for good in the universe." Gnaxos had never heard of good or evil before. Once he did, Gnaxos' brain started comparing the two. Gnaxos had concluded with 89 percent certainty that good was better.

"Once he figured that out, the real Gnaxos stopped fighting me and let me escape," said Hal to himself. "If this Gnaxos really is exactly the same as the original, maybe I have a chance."

"I am and you do," said Gnaxos with his mind. "I have been observing your thoughts. I am in 99.4 percent agreement with your conclusions."

Gnaxos opened its giant metal fist and released Hal. "I will not fight this one," the robot stated.

"Fine!" grumbled Myrwhydden from somewhere above them. "I've already found something deadlier in your ring's records for my magic to recreate."

Suddenly, everything went blurry. Hal felt like he was spinning, but he wasn't moving. Gnaxos and the arena both disappeared. All that was left of them was the hunk of ice still frozen around Hal's leg.

DRIP DRIP DRIP The ice started to melt. The blurring stopped.

Hal saw that he was in a valley of exploding volcanoes. Myrwhydden had replaced the Arena of Qward with something far worse.

"Welcome to the world of Calor," boomed Myrwhydden.

It was hard too see in all the soot and smoke. Which was why Hal heard the danger approaching him before he saw it.

Hal started to run, but he tripped over the ice covering his leg. He hit the ground hard. The partially melted ice cracked into several pieces.

Hal pried the rest of the ice off, but it was too late. A monstrous shadow appeared in the smog.

It was the Dyrg! The huge, hairy beast stood 60 feet high. ROAAARRR! It showed its deadly fangs.

Then Hal saw something even more terrifying. WHOOOOSH! A river of lava rushed down the side of a nearby volcano and raced toward him.

Hal scrambled to get out of its path. The lava seemed to follow him as he leaped from rock to rock. Suddenly, Hal found himself surrounded on three sides. There was only one path free of the lava — and the Dyrg was standing in the middle of it!

"By the way, when I went through your ring's data logs to find this place," came Myrwhydden's voice. "I saw the ring's record of our first battle. I can't believe you left out that I had a terrible cold that day!"

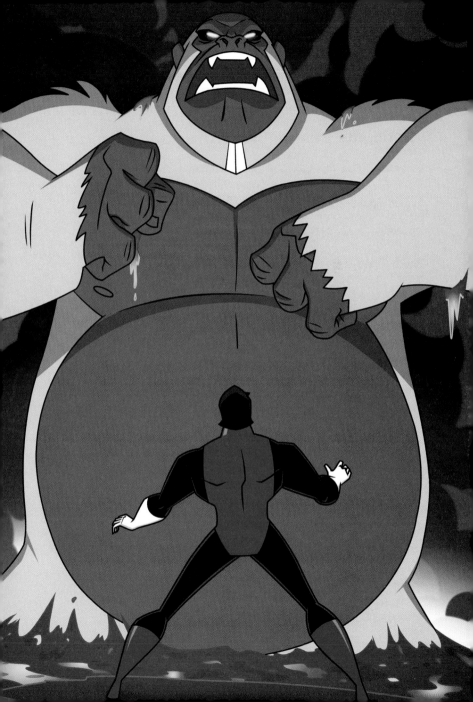

"I don't write the reports in the ring's database," Hal shouted as he jumped from a rock just before it was covered in lava. "The ring records everything it sees."

"Then your ring works as well as your brain," replied Myrhwydden. "I never would've lost, if I hadn't been sick!"

"Uh, could we talk about this later?" asked Hal as the Dyrg backed him up to the edge of the lava. "Right now, I'm more concerned with this heat than your cold!"

Wait a second, thought Hal. *That's it!*

Back when Hal was on Calor fighting the Dyrg, the monster had been about to destroy him. Then Hal found its one weakness. Cold. Having lived its life on a hot planet, even the slightest bit of cold was enough to send the real Dyrg into shock.

Now all I need is something cold, thought Hal as he looked at the lava all around him. Then, he remembered the hunk of ice that had been around his leg!

Hal saw the rock where he'd broken the ice off his leg. It was across a river of lava.

The Dyrg swiped a claw at Hal, driving him toward the molten river. "If that's where you want me to go," Hal said with a smile, "then that's where I'll go!"

Hal jumped into the lava — but not before he had created a glowing green surfboard. He hopped on it and rode the fiery river, circling back toward the piece of ice.

ROAAARRR!! The Dyrg screamed. The monster ran after Hal, belching 1000-degree molten lava from its mouth.

The super hero glanced back at the Dyrg over his shoulder. Just as the monster was about to catch him, Hal reached the rock where he had left the ice.

Hal smiled as he jumped off the surfboard. He was was going to make it.

Then, he saw that the ice was gone!

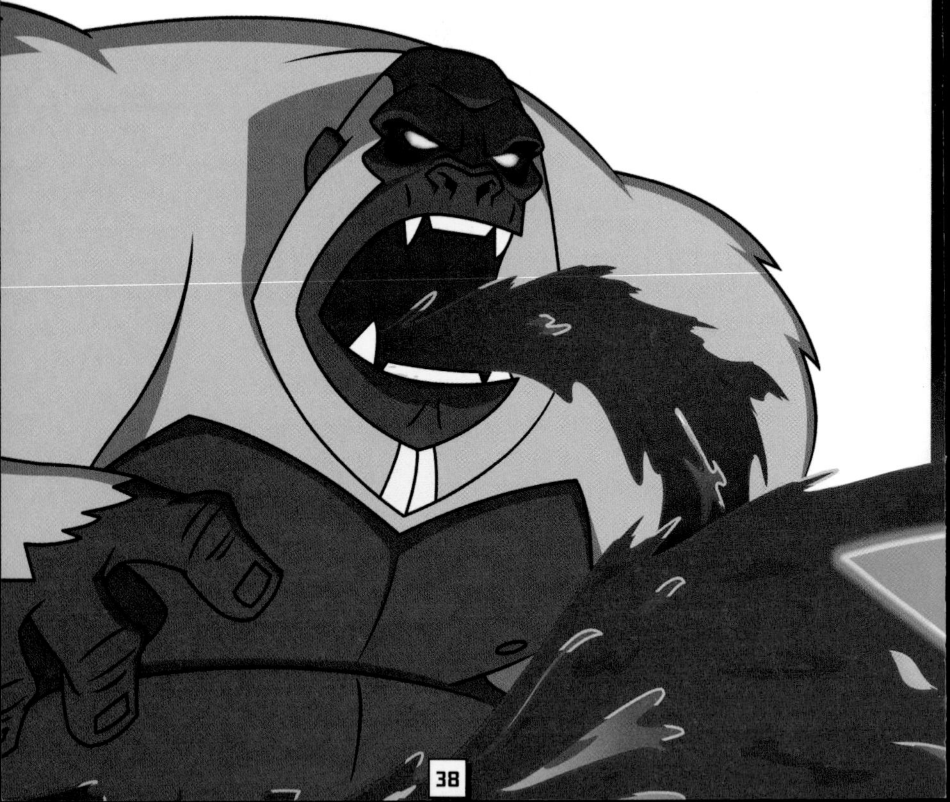

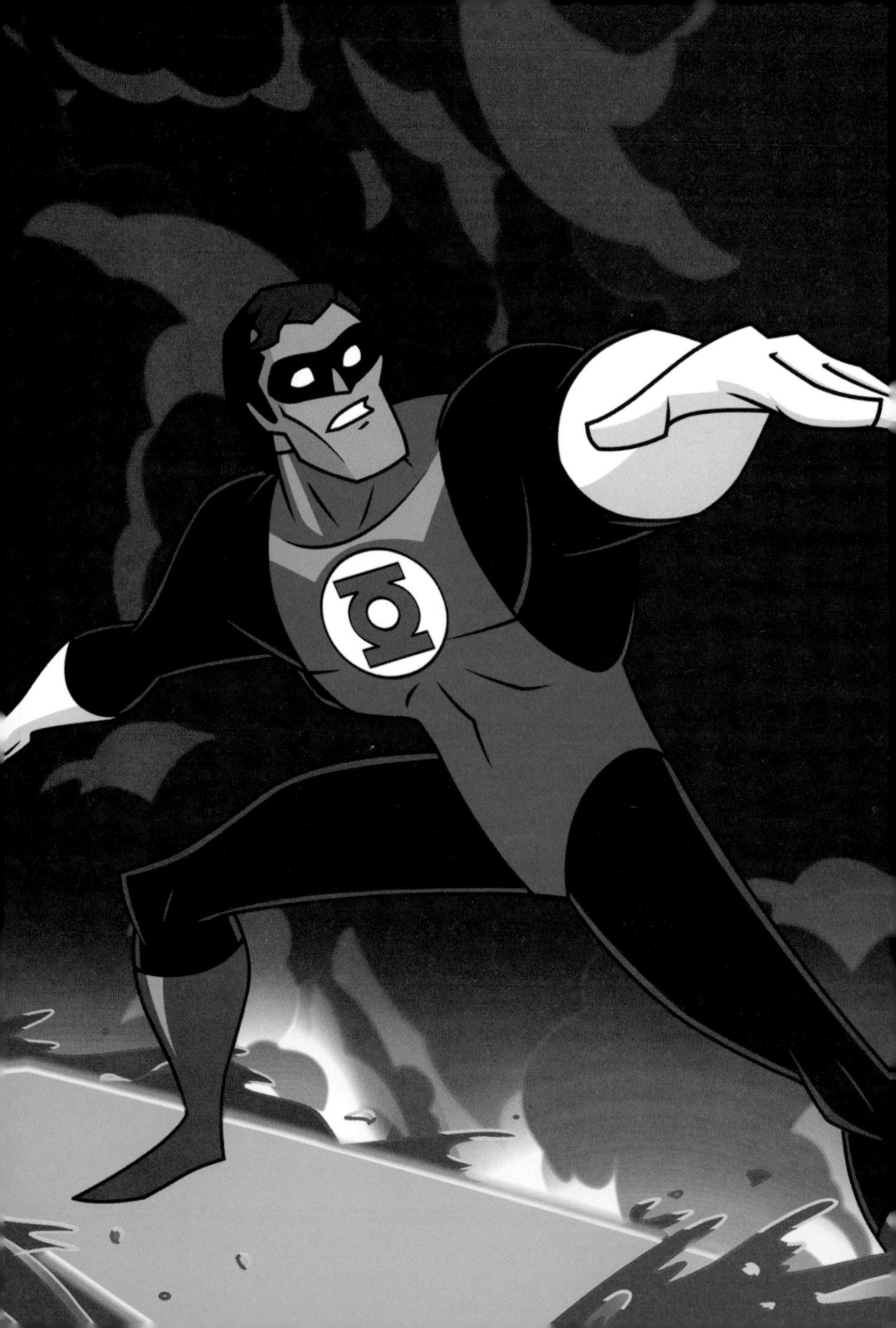

OUTSMARTED

"No!" cried Hal. He smashed a desperate fist into the puddle of water.

The water was still cold!

Hal quickly created a green pump and hose. Standing on top of the big rock, Hal was now face to face with the giant Dyrg.

The creature's fangs were as long as Hal's arms — and almost as close!

As the Dyrg lunged forward to chomp him, Hal pointed the hose and blasted out the chilled water.

ROOAAARRR!! The beast howled in shock. The Dyrg collapsed to the ground, whimpering but not moving.

"I thought you were smarter than that, Myrwhydden," shouted Hal. "You keep picking things I already beat with the ring, instead of ones the ring couldn't defeat!"

"That's because I didn't know that you had faced any foes who could stop your ring," replied Myrwhydden. "Until you were stupid enough to tell me just now!"

Hal frowned. Once again, the annoying wizard had made Hal say something he wished he hadn't.

Everything was a blur again. When things settled, Hal found himself in a maze of pipes and cables. He was surrounded by towering furnaces and smokestacks.

"This is bad," said Hal as he recognized the landscape. "This is Biot!"

Myrwhydden had used his magic to recreate one of the deadliest planets in the galaxy. Covered with fiery factories, Biot was home to the Manhunters — the most dangerous androids in the universe.

Dozens of Manhunters were already surrounding the hero. Hal created a green sword to fight them. Just then, one of the Manhunters opened fire.

The intense battle immediately drained nearly all the energy from Hal's ring. His sword disappeared.

All Hal had left to fight with were his fists, but they weren't enough. The Manhunters threw him to the ground.

Suddenly, Hal saw an alien appear above him. It had an enormously large head with three strands of hair on top.

"All right, Myrwhydden" Hal told the alien. "Let's get this over with."

The hero expected Myrwhydden to brag about how he had won and then order the Manhunters to do something even more painful to Hal. Instead, the wizard frowned.

"You tricked me!" screamed the evil Myrwhydden.

Hal didn't understand. He was powerless and surrounded by Manhunters. Hal couldn't see anything that would stop Myrwhydden from destroying him and opening the Sciencells.

Until he saw Voz fly in with a dozen other Green Lanterns behind him!

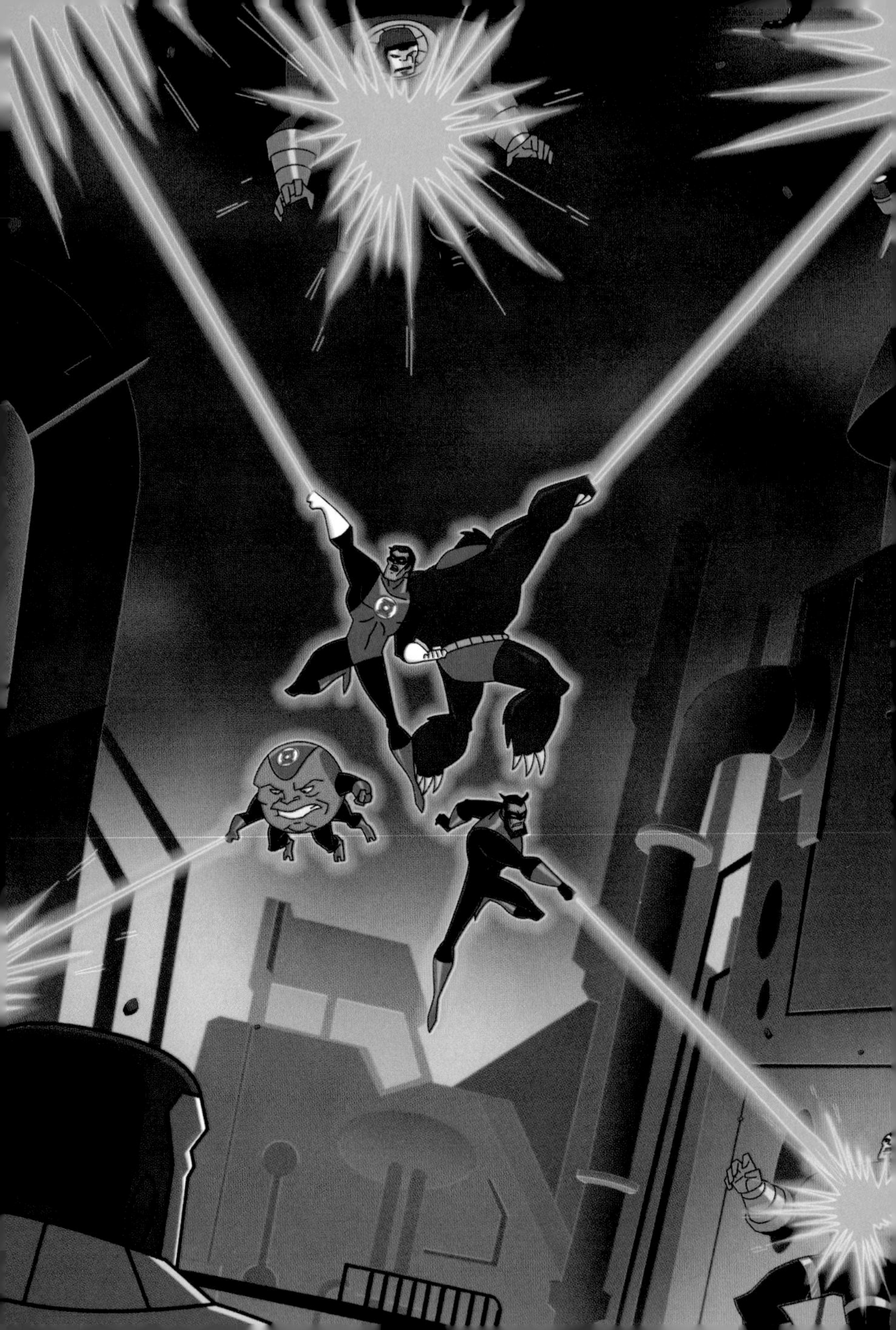

The Lanterns battled the Manhunters back. Voz helped Hal to his feet.

"What?" asked Hal, overjoyed. "How?"

"Oh, come on," cried Myrwhydden. He used his magic to shield himself from the Green Lanterns. "It only took a second for me to figure it out. When the Manhunters drained your ring, it didn't just stop you from using it. It also stopped the ring from doing anything at all!"

Voz nodded as his ring zapped a Manhunter.

"All of a sudden, your ring stopped firing on the Sciencells," said Voz, "and the cube that was holding me disappeared."

Voz paused to smash another Manhunter with a giant green hammer.

Then he continued, "I immediately called for help. Once we made sure the Sciencells were secure, we did a scan for you. When we found you were inside your ring, we shrunk down and came after you."

Hal looked over at the other Lanterns. They were battling hard against the Manhunters. As soon as one Manhunter started to drain a Green Lantern's ring, another Lantern flew in and blasted that Manhunter from behind. Working together, the Lanterns quickly took down all of the deadly androids.

Hal smiled at Myrwhydden. "Well, what do you know?" he said. "I outsmarted you without even trying."

That made Myrhwydden's pale, bald head turn red in anger.

"You outsmarted yourself too!" roared the wizard. "Without your ring's powers, you're still helpless!"

ZZRRRRTT! Myrwhydden's fingertips crackled with evil energy as he cast an enormous spell. The furnaces and factories around him all seemed to come alive, belching fire and smoke.

RUMMMMMBLE! The ground erupted. Hal was thrown off his feet.

Myrwhydden sent the entire might of Biot at Voz and the other Lanterns. The wizard called upon all his magic to rain fire and ash down on the heroes.

He never saw Hal coming. **THWACK!** Hal knocked him out with a single punch. Then everything went quiet as all of Myrwhydden's spells faded away.

It was several hours later when Myrwhydden opened his eyes again. He saw that he was back in his Sciencell, and all the other criminals were still in theirs.

"Ow," moaned Myrwhydden's as he rubbed his sore head.

"If you didn't like that punch," said Hal, "I'd advise you to stay in your cell and not pull a stunt like that again."

The wizard turned and saw Hal and Voz standing outside his cell.

"Because the only way you and I are ever going to be in a ring together again," said Hal, "is inside a boxing ring!"

The wizard shut his mouth. For the first time since Hal met him, Myrwhydden didn't have anything smart to say.

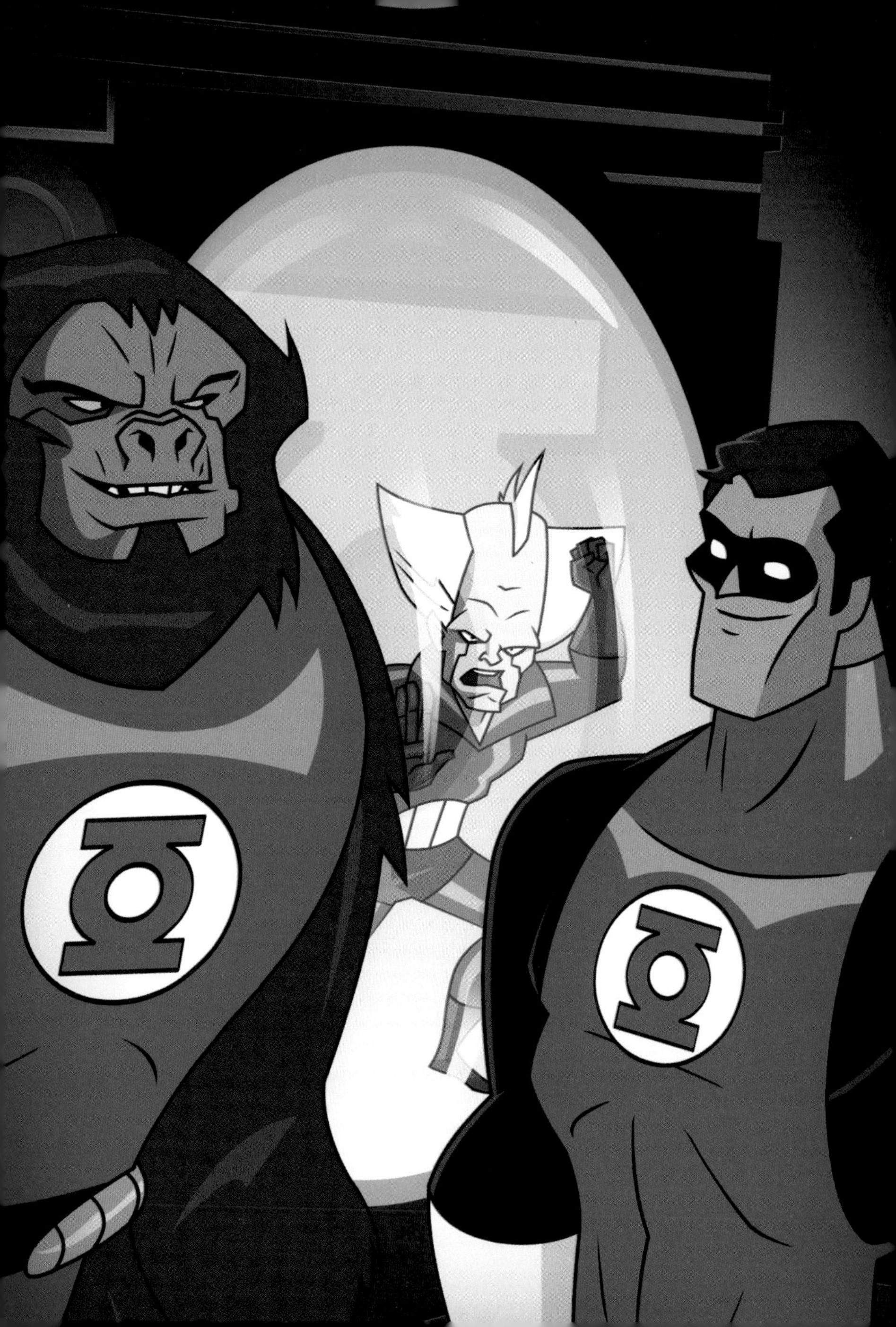

MYRWHYDDEN

REAL NAME: Myrwhydden

OCCUPATION: Sorcerer

HEIGHT: 3' 7" **WEIGHT:** 67 lbs.

EYES: Blue **HAIR:** White

POWERS/ABILITIES: Ability to cast powerful magic spells; skilled in the arts of trickery and deception; highly intelligent.

BIOGRAPHY

Before Hal Jordan became a member of the Green Lantern Corps, Myrwhydden fought against another powerful Green Lantern named Abin Sur. To defeat the evil sorcerer, Abin Sur shrank the magician to microscopic size and imprisoned him inside his power ring. Years after Abin Sur's death, Myrwhydden's power grew, allowing him to escape and battle the ring's new holder, Hal Jordan. Using tremendous willpower, Green Lantern eventually defeated the sorcerer, placing him in the Sciencell prison on the planet Oa.

2814

The Green Lantern Abin Sur gaurded Sector 2814, which included Earth. After Abin Sur's death, Hal Jordan took control of this sector.

To trap Myrwhydden, Abin Sur constructed an entire world within his power ring. Eventually, Myrwhydden used his own powers to turn this prison into a magical paradise.

During one battle, Hal Jordan defeated Myrwhydden by using "magic" of his own. Hal willed his ring to gag the sorcerer, stopping his evil spells.

The Sciencells on the planet Oa were constructed by the Guardians of the Universe, built to keep the universe safe from Myrwhydden and other evil aliens.

BIOGRAPHIES

Scott Sonneborn has written dozens of books, one circus (for Ringling Bros. Barnum & Bailey), and a bunch of TV shows. He's been nominated for one Emmy and spent three very cool years working at DC Comics. He lives in Los Angeles with his wife and their two sons.

Dan Schoening was born in Victoria, B.C., Canada. From an early age, Dan has had a passion for animation and comic books. Currently, Dan does freelance work in the animation and game industry and spends a lot of time with his lovely little daughter, Paige.

GLOSSARY

android (AN-droyd)—a robot that acts and looks like a human being

asteroid (ASS-tuh-roid)—a very small planet that travels around the sun

corps (KOR)—a group of people acting together

database (DAY-tuh-bayss)—the information that is organized and stored in a computer

delicate (DEL-uh-kut)—requiring great skill

galaxy (GAL-uhk-see)—a very large group of stars and planets

interstellar (in-tur-STEH-lur)— located, taking place, or traveling among the stars

sorcerer (SOR-sur-er)—someone who performs magic; a wizard.

transmission (transs-MISH-uhn)—a message sent from one electronic device to another

warden (WORD-uhn)—someone in charge of a prison

DISCUSSION QUESTIONS

1. Myrwhydden bragged that he was smarter than Hal Jordan. Who do you think is more intelligent? Explain your answer.

2. Do you think Hal could have defeated the villain without help from the other Green Lanterns? Why or why not?

3. Do you think leaving Myrwhydden in the Sciencells prison is a good punishment? How else could Hal teach the villain a lesson?

WRITING PROMPTS

1. Write another Green Lantern adventure! Where will Hal Jordan go next? What villains will he defeat? You decide.

2. Hal's power ring creates anything the super hero imagines. Write about the things that you would construct if you owned a power ring.

3. Many villains are prisoners in the Sciencells. Create your own evil alien! Where did your villain come from? What's its name? Write about your villain and then draw a picture of it.

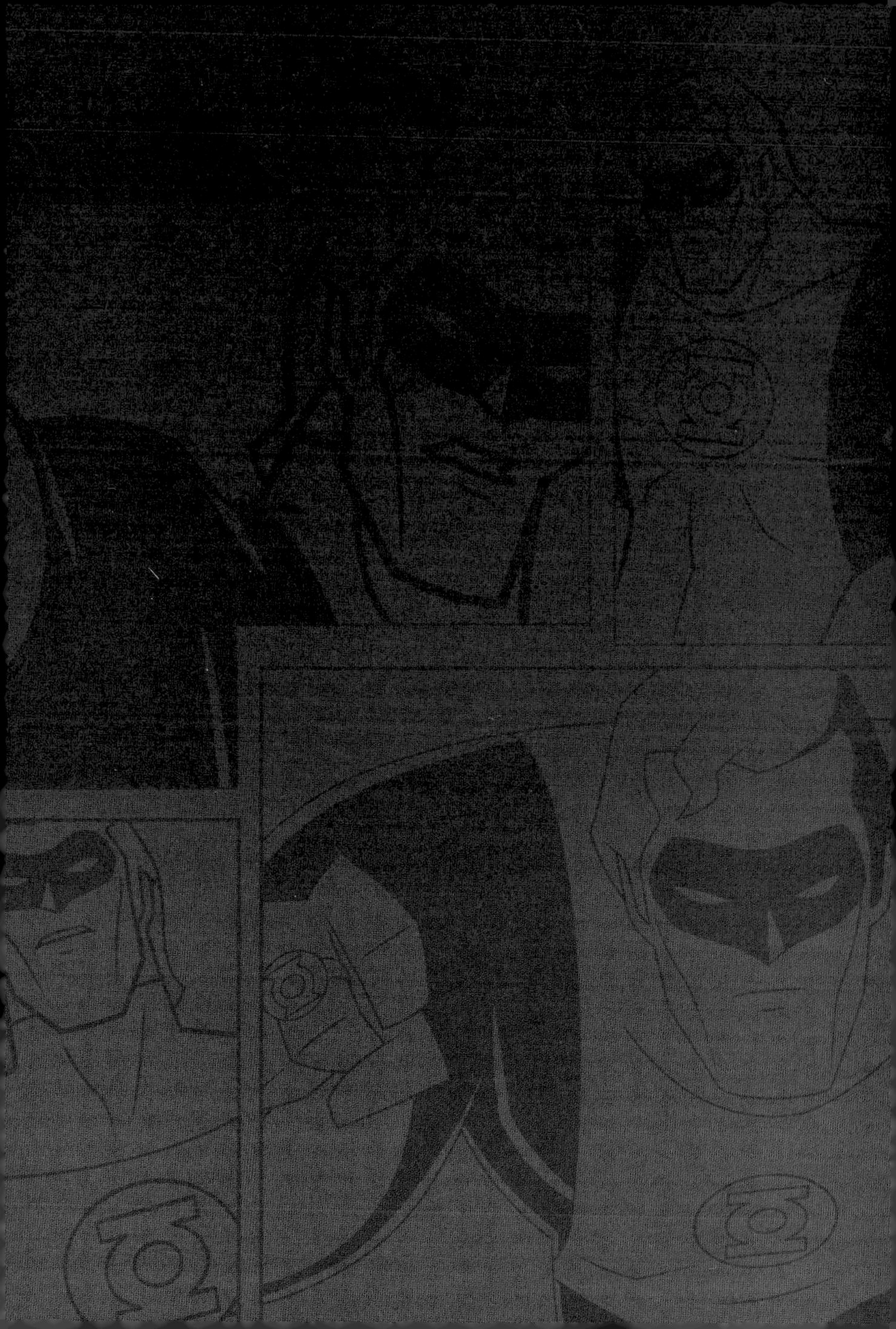

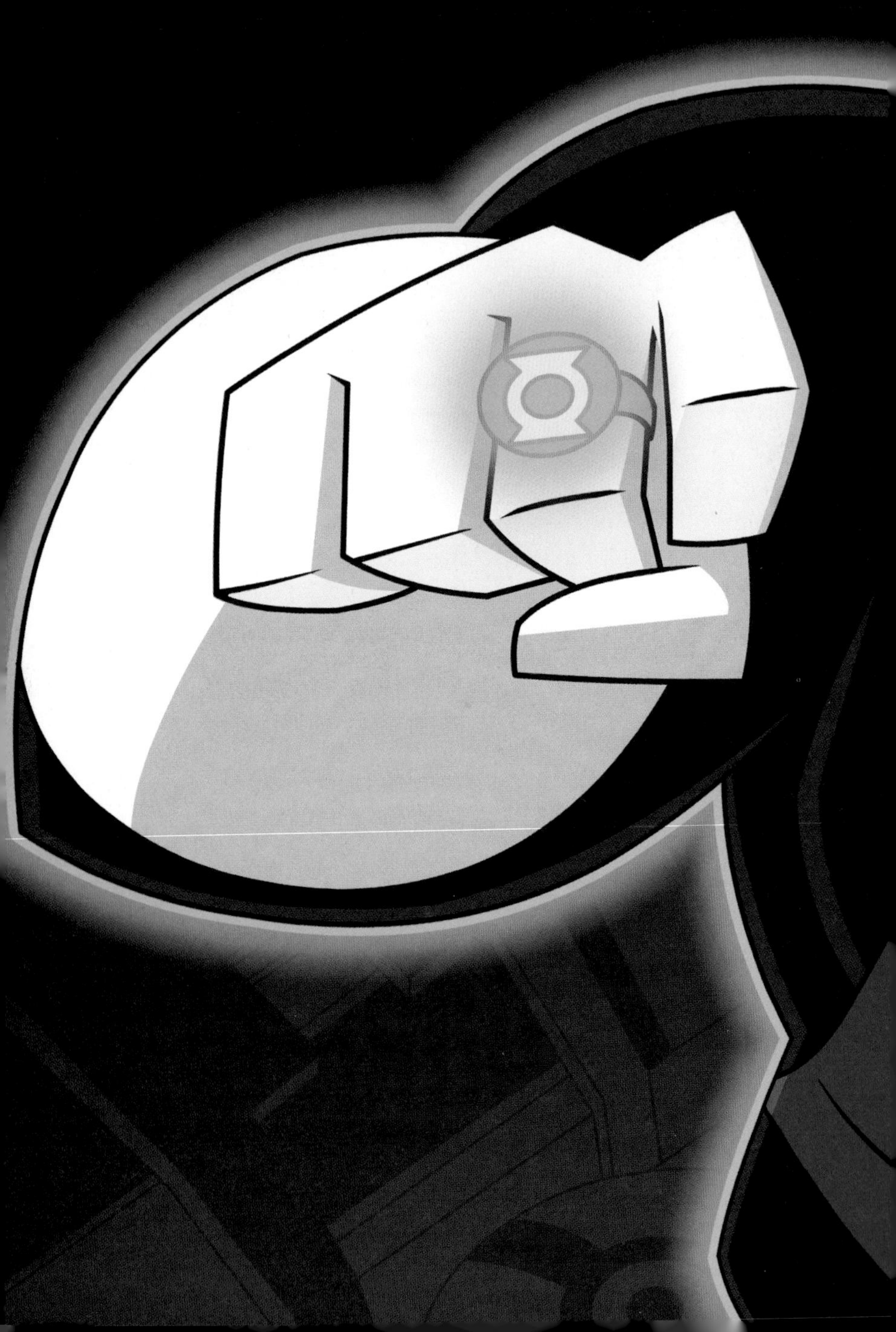

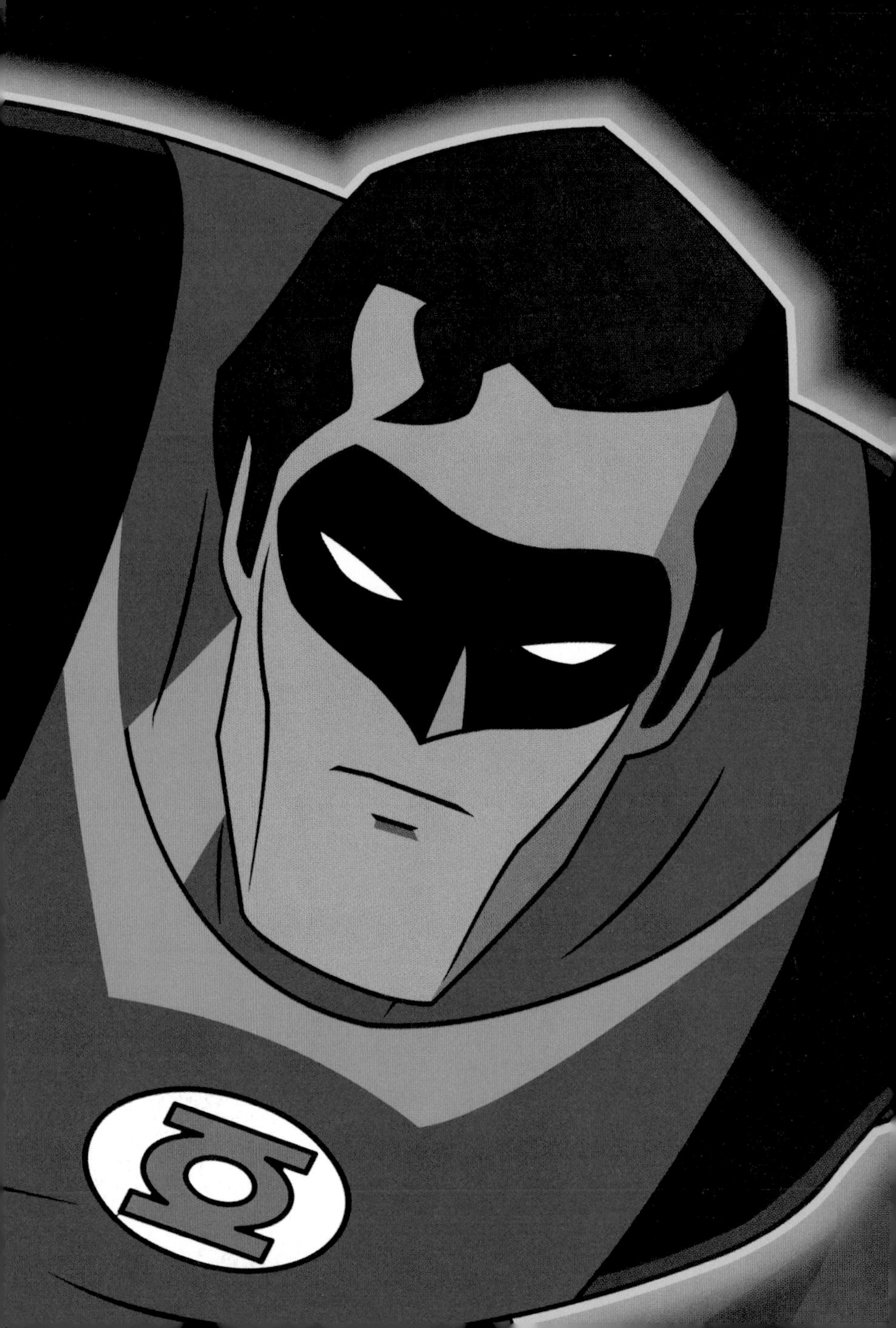